SPEED OF LIGHT

Dramatis Personae

Characters/Cast

G1.......... Stuart Mansell

G2.......... Tony Hendon

Jenia........ Jenia Emmanuelle

Vincent.... Vincent Hall

Thomas.... Alex Hall

The Narrator... ?

SUMMARY

Thomas (15) and Vincent (13) are two brothers. One day they decide to run away from a broken home. They land on a small island off the South Coast of England to escape their current reality.

On the island they discover a huge, derelict and abandoned warehouse and they are on their way to explore it with only a lighter.

G1 is a small-time crook, who lives inside a washroom in the abandoned warehouse. G1 believes that he has a girlfriend and dreams of her.

Jenia is a young girl, 22, mean and vulgar. She has spent most of her life inside a housing estate.

G1 works occasionally, he jumps on the ferry to the mainland to steal from people. G1 is in his thirties and he has a severe drug problem. He has a mate, Kid or G2, a small-time crook who pops in on various occasions. Like Thomas he is also obsessed with one book entitled "Speed of Light". When he is not a small-time crook, he reads it all the time. Unlike G1 he hasn't got a drug problem. G1 often dreams about his girlfriend and some of his dreams occurring at the speed of light cross the boundaries between dream and reality. One such moment is an intimate sex scene between the two protagonists that may or may not have been real. Even in the film the viewers were left wondering if the protagonists were willing participants or if G1 indeed raped his girlfriend.

The two brothers arrive in the warehouse one fine day in the summer and remain there until the early hours of the next day.

Exhausted after a long, frantic and scary search for some adventure from the basement to the top floor, they fall asleep on the stairs. Later they bump into G1. From then on, the nightmare begins. The two brothers are being held hostage throughout the night in a violent and bloody ordeal. By the morning the youngest brother transforms himself from a terrified child into a ferocious, vengeful killer and takes control of the situation.

They manage to escape; Thomas is severely wounded but alive leaving G1 dead behind.

Parallel to the story, Thomas, the older brother, is obsessed by a science fiction novel and spends most of his time telling and narrating the content to his brother and ends up annoying him in the process.

The film opens with Thomas reading his book called: "Speed of Light" over a series of images.

Synopsis

Two brothers land on an island and discover a huge and derelict warehouse. They discover what could happen at the speed of light. It's the tale of two stories colliding throughout an entire night. Two stories lived at the same time, but with a slightly different content.

Scene 1: "Prologue:

The Origins of Light"

The film begins and ends from within a giant ray of light. The whole screen is immersed into a ray of light with various degrees of intensity.

Thomas is reading his book called: "Speed of Light" aloud seated on the upper deck of the ferry in the middle of the sea with Vincent by his side. They are only seen toward the end of the scene.

At the beginning, the narration is read over a series of graphics. The graphics are extracted from a prism of light and displayed on the screen like a slideshow.

Thomas

The distance from Earth to the Moon is about 239 000 miles. This is extremely fast and indeed in theory nothing can travel faster than the speed of light. Life seems to travel from one place to another instantaneously. When the light is switched on there is no delay between when we first see the light and when the light illuminates the far end of the room. Our brain is slow to detect the rays of light that appear from the bulb like a wave washing over the room. In space light seems slow, very slow…

Pause.

The distance light can travel by a year. The delay caused by the speed of light can sometimes be noticed here on earth during telephone calls. Long distance calls that have been rooted over one or more space satellites and caused half a second or so delay between the speaker and the listener. All electro-magnetic radiation between radio waves and x rays can travel at the speed of light and into space, speeding at 300 000 kilometers per second. We can even predict the wave link of the electro-magnetic wave if we know the time it takes to change to what is known as the speed of light.

Thomas is now seen on the ferry, sitting and reading his book with his brother Vincent seated by his side.

Time is called the period T of the wave. By multiplying the period of the speed of light we can determine the wave link of any waves thus known as the speed of light.

Light may be seen and interpreted in different ways by different people. One person may see an event or another person differently than you see. Light can play tricks with your eyes. You may see something or someone else and it might be the reflection of your imagination triggered by the rays of the speed of light seen by oneself.

Scene 2: "Across the sea"

The Narrator

In the main port there are only a few ships and ferries. Not many people land on this part of the world; only fishermen mainly and the occasional tourists. In any given decade in England, each location tends to bear a different status. One decade any place is a busy, affluent and trendy spot and another decade it's complete devastation. No one wants to know the place.

One morning, two brothers in need of some adventure boarded a ship to a mysterious island off the South coast of England.

Thomas is obsessed with a book called "Speed of Light". He has been reading it for the past two years. He has taken his book on the journey and keeps on reading some chapters to his brother. It's a good two hours journey to the island but it is a nice day. The waves tend to be very high this morning and the wind blows slowly over the ship. The ship is a passenger's ship and a ferry but it's empty. The only passengers are the two brothers.

The more the ship glides over the water and the more the wind tends to blow. The wind seems to communicate with the two brothers what lies ahead in their journey. It's almost like a symphony of noises, music and sound with images of this future being projected by the wind.

Scene 3: "Meet G1 and G2"

G1 is fast asleep inside one of the toilets, on the toilet seat, the door is shut. G2 is knocking then banging at the door to wake G1 up.

G2

Knocking at the door

Wake up, man, bloody wake up!

G1

G1 is still in a trance, his eyes wide shut

Wot? Wot?

G2

Banging at the door

Wake up!

G1

What about the kids?

G2

What fucking kids?

G1

Them lot by the sink!

G2

There isn't anyone there. There is never anyone here.

G1

It is bloody here!

G2

I'm off G, I'm out of here brov' (brother)!

G1

Don't leave me; I'm always on my own!

G2

That's your fucking problem!

G1

You always said you were gonna leave me but you never do.

G2 leaves the washroom, the warehouse and the story.

Scene 4: "Eat Speed"

G1 is having a conversation with G2 in the washroom.

G1

Fucking what? Fucking speed? You're a black kid and you can't even nick fuck at all! You can't even fuck a girl without talking to her. Always reading that fucking book! You eat speed, you don't fucking read it!

Scene 5: "The House"

The two brothers are wandering around inside the house.

It's in the middle of the afternoon and they feel already exhausted by their journey. They both fall asleep on the stairs. The sun's rays have penetrated their thoughts and from then on, the adventure begins.

It's getting dark but they are not afraid of the dark. They wander around the house in the dark. For a while they do not speak to each other. The dialogue is only happening inside their heads. Eventually when it becomes too dark, Vincent switches his lighter on.

Thomas

My parents are a bunch of wankers. Why do parents have children when they end up dumping them or abusing them?

Vincent

My brother is ok. He had a girlfriend once. What he doesn't know is that I went out with her too.

Thomas

There's always something to do inside an abandoned house.

Not like at home.

Vincent

I'm getting bored of this shitty place. Nothing ever happens there, you wait and wait and nothing. It's a hell hole.

Thomas

I wish I could come here with my girlfriend. I can think of a few things we can do but I've lost her. I'm stuck with my brother. He's only thirteen.

Vincent

I still see my brother's girlfriend but he doesn't know. I've been out with girls for a while now. I'm not doing anything heavy but pretty nice all the same.

Thomas

I might push my brother down the stairs that might
scare him off. It's always difficult to meet with my
girlfriend. When we meet it's always in a corner
somewhere, not in my flat my parents wouldn't allow it.

Vincent

When I met my brother's girlfriend, it was always for an
hour or two at least. We used to hide inside a shopping
center somewhere where no one could see us.

Thomas

I'm glad my girlfriend left me. I never knew what she
wanted. I always had to force her to do things. She
didn't want to do anything at first, but then she changed
her mind again.

Vincent

My brother's girlfriend never wants to do anything. I
always have to ignore her and always have to do what
grabs my fancy. You have to be forceful though.

The two brothers are now talking to each other

Vincent

Where's your book?

Thomas

No, I've got it with me

Vincent

Shit. That's one thing you could have lost... bloody book.

This is because of your stupid book we're stuck in here!

Back to their respective thoughts

Thomas

According to my book, there is always light around even when it's dark. The light is invisible to the naked eye.

Vincent

At least when it's dark my brother can't read his fucking book. Why read about light when you're stuck inside a house or a book, in this case.

What I really miss is when I'm on top of her and I end up on the floor. I'm always on top of her. I always come out quickly in one shot. With my brother's girlfriend we always keep our clothes on. It is much better. Sometimes my trousers end up on the floor or by my feet. I always have to force her to either sit on a chair or on a toilet seat.

Thomas

It's not in a place like this that I'm likely to meet my girlfriend.

Vincent

My brother's girlfriend always wears a short white dress.

She's barely taller than I am.

Thomas is trying to scare Vincent and in doing so he is pushing his brother from behind.

Vincent

Ah! Fucking wanker!

Pause.

Vincent

What's there?

Thomas

It's only the door

Vincent

What's there? What's there?

Thomas

Stupid idiot! That's only the door

Vincent

Over here!

Thomas

What?

Vincent

Over here!

Thomas

There's nothing over there!

Vincent

Over here!

Thomas

What?

Vincent

There's something over there... There, move quickly!

Thomas

There is nothing over there! Stop saying this.

Vincent

Come quickly in here!

Thomas

What?

Vincent

There's something over there...

Thomas

I'm not coming over there! **Short pause**

Vincent

I need the loo

Thomas

Yeah, yeah!

Vincent

I really need the loo!

Thomas

Don't let me stop you

Vincent

In case you haven't noticed it is pitch black over here

Thomas

I have never been here before!

Vincent

I'm doing it in here

Vincent urinates in the dark

Thomas

Fuck! You pissed over me!

Vincent

I can't see anything

Thomas

That's no reason

Vincent

I've never done it in the dark before. Anyway, it's done now. Where do we go now?

Thomas

Straight up!

Vincent falls on the floor

Vincent

Ah...

Thomas

What are you doing here?

Vincent

I fell

Thomas

You're so clumsy!

Vincent

It's bloody dark...

Whilst they wander in the dark G1 is well aware of their presence. The two brothers have been loud

enough. He is waiting for them, halfway through the stairs with a gun in his hands. Further up the stairs there are some windows and it's now in the early hours of the morning; there is some dim light around.

The two brothers bumped into G1 on a next turn in the stairs.

G1

Don't fucking move! Don't fucking move!

The two brothers obey. They are directed to move upstairs into the main washroom.

Scene 6: "Gun Scene"

G1

Why are you here?

Vincent

What?

Trembling

G1

Fuck off boyo! Who's got the fucking gun?

Vincent

You!

G1

Too fucking right!

Vincent

Hmm

G1

So, who else is with you?

Vincent

No one...

G1

Don't fucking lie to me!

Vincent

My brother

G1

Who's fucking brother?

Vincent

He is my brother *pointing at Thomas with his left thumb*

G1

Talking to Thomas

Move your fucking ass over here!

G1

Who else?

Vincent

No one I told you

G1

Shut up. Shut it!

Thomas

No one else!

G1

I don't fucking believe you fucking mouth!

Vincent

It's your...choice!

G1

Trembling

What fucking choice?

Vincent

Your problem...

G1

What fucking problem? Do you want a fucking bullet in your fucking 'ead? (Head)

Vincent

Then What?

G1

Then What? I don't fucking believe this! Now who else is with ya?

Thomas

Just us

Vincent

Soon after

The three of us

G1

What fucking three?

Vincent

You and us!

G1

No one else?

Thomas

No one else!

Vincent

What do you want from us?

G1

Smart ass, I ask the questions. Shut it! Shut your fucking mouth!

Small pause: 10 seconds. View of everyone's face.

Vincent

Vincent breaks the silence.

Are you scared?

G1

Fuck You!

Thomas

We won't tell anyone

G1

Getting very agitated

Shut up! Shut the fuck up!

A deep silence immerses the washroom for about a minute. The anxiety is clearly visible on everyone's face. G1 is still pointing the gun at Vincent's head.

Vincent

Vincent breaks the silence.

This is leading us nowhere.

G1

Shut it!

Vincent

Are you scared?

G1

What? Who's scared? Who's got the gun here?

Thomas

You!

G1 turns his face on his left toward Thomas and he is still pointing with the gun.

G1

Right! There's a bright ass over here!

Vincent

I'm...

G1

Turns his head back toward Vincent and he is still pointing with the gun.

Wot?

Vincent

Can I help?

G1

Wot?

Vincent

Do you need help?

G1

You, fucking smart kids! You think you've got it all. I worked my guts to get all this shit. Don't have fucking parents with fucking loads of 'dosh' to burn. This is mine and no one is fucking gonna take it from me. Fucking right?

Vincent

...Yes

G1

Looking at Thomas and still pointing with the gun

What's that?

Thomas

Yes, right...

G1

Grabs Thomas from the back of his shirt and points the gun toward his head.

Clear?

Thomas

Clear!

G1 pushes Thomas near the sink knocking his head over in the process and he falls unconscious on the floor. Thomas starts to bleed from the right side of his head. Vincent moves toward Thomas.

Vincent

Tom, are you, all right? Tom?

G1

G1 then seizes the opportunity to take the back of his gun and hits Vincent over his head with it. Vincent falls unconscious over Thomas. His head starts to bleed.

G1 is restless. He stands in front of the sink facing the mirror then stares at the floor where the two brothers lie unconscious. He grabs a cigarette, gets a lighter and nearly burns himself. He now smokes desperately. G1 looks at himself in the mirror and he is extremely angry. He looks at the window on his right-hand side then back at the two brothers. He then opens a can of beer:

Tenant Super Lager, the Downs and Outs favorite brew. He's slowly calming himself down.

G1 had another busy day. It's a good ten minutes since he knocked the two brothers unconscious and G1 is getting very tired. He suddenly grabs the gun, turns behind him and enters the toilet. He has a slash standing up. He's too tired to move. He slowly and painfully sits on the toilet seat with the gun in his hands and falls into another deep trance.

Scene 7: "G1's life on the floor"

The Narrator

G1 seldom travels to the mainland. He spends his entire time in the warehouse. He sleeps in the warehouse. He does whatever he wants to do. The house is his kingdom. No one can disturb him. No one can enter his kingdom without his approval. He only meets the people he wants to meet. He triggers the events; his events. He controls his own destiny. When he is hungry, he hunts for food in the warehouse, like any insect would do. He does it like an insect; half asleep half-awake almost in a state of complete trance.

He crawls on the floor. He smells the floor and licks the floor. When he sees some spiders or cockroaches; he squashes them with his punch then licks the floor.

There is plenty to be discovered inside an abandoned warehouse; some old furniture, books, pieces of clothing or newspapers. G1 acts and feels like a cockroach whether he thinks like one is another matter.

Sometimes, G1 has got a very peculiar way of washing himself. He scratches away the dust and the occasional itch and when he does it, it's like an erupted volcano: he scratches and scratches incessantly until he bleeds away, until there is almost no more blood left.

Blood always attracts rats and when G1 sees one, he grabs it by the tail and smashes the poor devil against the wall. Then he eats it. Just like that, screaming ferociously at the dead rat.

This is G1's life in his own kingdom on a deserted island.

Scene 8: "The Speed of Light"

The Narrator

Today G1 found a box of light bulbs in the house. He is very intrigued and excited as if he has never seen any. Maybe he never did. Inside his main living quarters, the washroom he is staring frantically at one of the bulbs. He turns the light bulb around and around and again in reverse. He looks at it in the mirror and sees himself in the mirror holding the light bulb. After a few seconds he gets into another rage and throws the light bulb on the floor. The noise of the broken light bulb is so deafening and yet G1 seems fascinated by it. He grabs another one then throws it on the floor. He pauses for a few seconds in order to enjoy the reverberation from the sound of the broken light. The sound seems to have triggered something inside his brain. He grabs another light bulb then he throws it again on the floor. He repeats the action with another one and another one until the box of light bulbs is finally empty. G1 is not happy. He groans, grits his rotten teeth or what's left and kicks the wall with his feet.

He's now searching for some cigarettes but cannot find any. By then he is completely exhausted. He is going back to the washroom, to the toilet seat nearby and falls into a semi-coma.

G1 had another busy day.

Scene 9: "Romp"

G1 sits on the toilet seat, his trousers and underwear are on the floor and his girlfriend sits on his lap wearing a tiny skirt, almost revealing what's underneath.

G1 is somewhat rough when fondling Jenia. Jenia is struggling to cope. She's asking him to let go but G1 refuses and he is becoming more and more obsessed by his actions, unable to respond or let go of Jenia.

Turning in circles, rotating sideways on the toilet seat, G1 is in full swing. Jenia screams some more and G1 responds accordingly.

G1

Stay still! What's the matter with ya?

Eventually G1 manages to penetrate inside Jenia's female organ, located underneath her tiny white skirt, covering what is actually going on as if someone would be watching.

Jenia's strides G1's male organ against her will, G1's legs are in the middle and Jenia's legs are on the side. Jenia can't help by hugging G1, feeling unable to detach herself from the current penetration.

G1's screams are getting louder and louder and so is

Jenia's. G1's screams edge toward orgasm and Jenia's toward desperation.

Jenia

You're hurting me!

G1

Fucking stop moving!

Jenia

Stop it!

G1

I say stop. Stop what? Come here!

Jenia

Noooo....

In a moment of weakness, G1 lets go of Jenia. Jenia seizes the moment to escape only to be grabbed two seconds later by G1.

G1 is very angry. He screams and swears blue murder at Jenia. He then tries to stand up and pushes Jenia aside in the process.

His T-shirt is covering his male organ. His trousers and underwear are still on his feet and he pushes Jenia outside the cubicle toward the corridor. G1 pushes Jenia on the floor and Jenia ends up semi-conscious, lying on her back.

G1 jumps over her body and lies over her. G1's back side is now in full display. It leaves nothing to the imagination: the front of his body, his male organ, is obviously fully lodged inside Jenia's organ. G1 is pushing deeper and deeper inside Jenia's organ and by now Jenia has regained consciousness and is desperately trying to move away and the more she does, the more she amplifies G1's excitement.

Jenia

No...

G1

Fuck you!

Do as I say or you'll end up like the two kids over there...

With his right thumb, G1 is showing the wall where he can see the two brothers

Jenia

Jenia looks at the wall but cannot see anyone

What Kids?

G1 firmly believes that the two brothers, Thomas and Vincent are lying unconscious on the floor.

G1

These kids…

Pointing again at the wall

Jenia

There are no kids!

G1

Now I give the orders

Jenia

You stink!

G1

Yeah just what you like

Jenia

You're no one. You're a ghost in an empty space!

G1 suddenly feels a deep sense of release. He feels completely worn out, beaten and yet he ejaculates inside Jenia.

Jenia screams and screams some more.

Jenia

Screaming

This place is like a graveyard.

This place is like a graveyard.

Scene 10: "On the floor"

G1 gets up grabs his trousers with his left hand and then he grabs Jenia's hair with his right hands. Jenia is still lying on the floor and is too terrified to move. She is then pushed again inside the toilet's cubicle.

When seen from behind, as if the walls had eyes and if they could see the back of Jenia entering the toilet; her small white dress stuck nearer to her breast would reveal a full, rounded bottom. This clarifies what was on display in front of her whilst G1 was penetrating her.

If her butt was naked it means that Jenia's female organ was free from any clothing. The bright view of her rear end hereby clarifies the situation, just in case the walls had eyes but no ears.

As soon as G1 is seated back on the toilet seat with Jenia's on his lap, G1 is replaying in his mind the first time Jenia has entered the toilet. Another twenty minutes of agonizing ordeal for Jenia but lust and passion for G1 until he is fully asleep, leaving Jenia free to run away.

Jenia does run away and G1 continues with his dream still believing that the two brothers have been knocked over by the sink and the brothers still believe that they have been knocked unconscious.

<u>Scene 11: "The Killing"</u>

The two brothers knocked out on the floor are still lying down by the sink.

Vincent wakes up and asks his brother if he is ok. He tries to wake his brother up.

Vincent

Thomas, Thomas, you're ok? We must go now!

Tom, wake up!

Thomas is struggling to wake up. He is still numb but he is carried away by his brother.

As soon as they have left the washroom and the door has been slammed behind them, the noise wakes G1 up.

G1

With a desperate and agonizing tone in his voice

Hey, come back, come back!

G1 is pursuing the two brothers up the stairs, shooting indiscriminately in the dark, from floor to floor.

Come back, Come back!

The two brothers didn't go upstairs in the labyrinthine warehouse but downstairs toward the main entrance.

Half way through the door, Vincent suddenly leaves Thomas on the floor and rushes back upstairs.

With a vengeful look in his eyes, determined to carry out what he has set out to achieve, Vincent reaches the top of the staircase. He grabs his lighter to shine a light and to guide his way into the darkness.

He is hiding behind a wall and G1 is hiding behind another. Vincent has no fears, he feels completely empowered by a sudden unknown force. G1 on the other hand is panic stricken, mortified in this complete darkness. He can hear some noises and can feel a presence but even with a gun in his hand he feels completely insecure and trapped into an impossible situation.

In one split second the G1 and Vincent meet. Vincent's lighter burns G1's face.

G1 drops his gun and falls on the floor. Vincent finds the gun and he uses it to kill G1. It's all over. G1 has been shot dead.

He is lying down on the floor on his back.

Scene 12: "The Escape"

G1 is free to return to the land of the nod whilst Vincent is free to fetch his brother, to leave this frightening and desperate warehouse; down the stairs again, five floors down carrying his brother, still semi unconscious. They are using a wobbly, shrieking 1920's style lift, out of the house, out to freedom and back to the port, to the land of the living.

<u>Scene 13: "At the port"</u>

Thomas and Vincent are in the washrooms at the sea port washing their hands.

They are both staring at the huge oblong mirror in front of them for a few minutes, wondering if it was all for real.

<u>Scene 14: "What really happened?"</u>

The two brothers are sitting on the ferry waiting to depart.

Vincent

How fast does the wind blow then?

Thomas

As fast as 'it' can, as fast as the speed of light

Vincent

You're right about one thing though…

Thomas

What?

Vincent

Everything can happen at the speed of summer lightning, at the speed of light. I'm not sure if anything happened anymore.

Thomas

What happened? I can still feel it but I can't remember it.
I can but I'm not sure how it happened. It's all in the
waves.

Vincent

That's not in your book?

Thomas

No...

*The ferry has left the island. They are now in the sea and
Vincent and Thomas are continuing their conversation.*

Vincent

But you're not even bruised anymore...

Thomas

No. That went away...

Vincent

Your blood 'is' gone

Thomas

Yeah. Just about, just a trace

They have now moved on the upper deck of the ferry.

Vincent

It's like if millions of things happened in that house. I'm not sure which one is real and which one is not and which one we've actually seen...

Thomas

So, what happened then?

The whole story suddenly flashes in front of their eyes.

The whole story lived inside the house, on the sea, backwards and in reverse.

Was it a dream? If yes, how come everything seems so real? Thomas was wounded and bled, this is real.

Thomas can still 'see it' and 'feel it' but it is almost gone. Gone with the wind on a journey to a mysterious island where there is a house inhabited by a man who believes he has a girlfriend called Jenia and a partner in crime called G2.

Scene 15: "Epilogue"

The Narrator

There are many origins about the speed of light. Some have argued that it is triggered by an unknown and superior force somewhere in deep space. This force created light and the light in turn created the planets and life as we know it.

Everything happens at the speed of light, at the speed of summer lightning, in an instant, inside a Nano-second.

We believe that it is slow, that life triggered by the speed of light moves like a snail gliding over the grass. But in real terms it isn't. Everything moves in an instant, so fast that light plays tricks with our eyes. We may believe that an event has occurred, that we have seen something, that we have lived a new adventure but in reality, it's only the light that has created our own illusion, entertainment.

Thomas and Vincent are two brothers. One day they decide to run away from a broken home. They land on a small island off the South Coast of England to escape their current reality.

On the island they discover a huge, derelict and abandoned warehouse and they are on their way to explore it with only a lighter.

G1 is a small-time crook, who lives inside a washroom in an abandoned warehouse. G1 has a girlfriend or believes he has. He dreams that she visits him from time to time.

Jenia is young, mean and vulgar. She has spent most of her life living inside a London housing estate.

G1 works occasionally, he jumps on the ferry to the mainland to steal whatever he can. G1 is in his thirties and has a severe drug problem. He has a friend, Kid or G2, a small-time crook who sometimes pops into his story. Unlike G1, G2 hasn't got a drug problem.

The two brothers arrive in the warehouse one summer and remain there until the early hours of the next day.

Exhausted after a long, frantic and scary search for some adventure from the basement to the top floor, they fall asleep on the stairs. Later they bump into G1. From then on, the nightmare begins. The two brothers are being held hostage throughout the night in a violent and bloody ordeal. By the morning the younger brother transforms himself from a terrified child into a ferocious, vengeful killer and takes control of the situation.

They manage to escape; Thomas is severely wounded but alive leaving G1 dead behind.

Parallel to the story, Thomas, the older brother, is

obsessed by a science fiction novel entitled "Speed of Light" and spends most of his time telling and narrating the content to his brother.

"Nothing is faster than light: it travels at 300,000 kilometers per second! The light from the moon reaches us in about one second.

Light is an electromagnetic wave. Its spectrum reaches from infrared, a wavelength longer than visible light, all the way to the x-ray region. The only range of light visible to the human eye is very small: wavelengths between around 700 and 400 Nanometers – from red to ultraviolet light. If we allow light to fall on a prism, we can look through the light and see the color spectrum. We can bring together red, green and blue light. Our brain sees the mixture as 'white light'. This is the basis of display technology. ``

What happened? What really happened? Was it all a dream or a nightmare? What are we to believe, to remember?

Is there anything to believe?

Everything happens at the speed of light, at the speed of summer lightning, in an instant, inside a nanosecond in one billionth of a second.

There is a clear correlation between the waves in the oceans and the speed of light: it's all in the intensity, the force and the determination of the action.

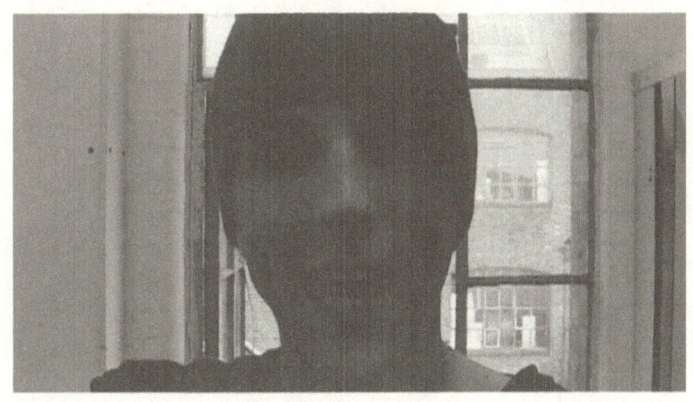

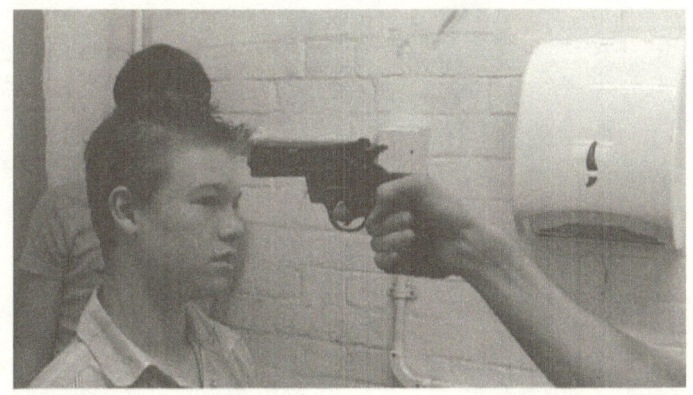

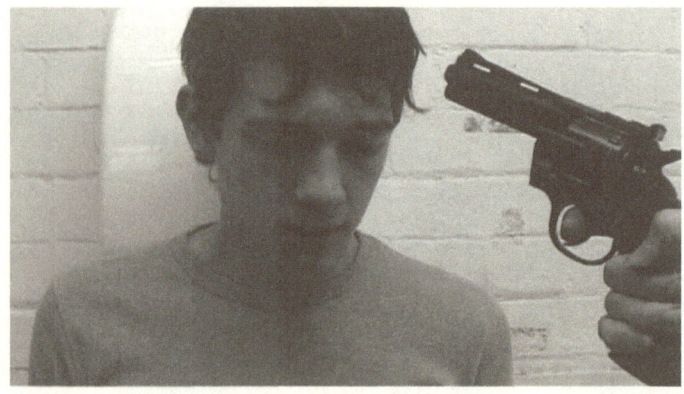

Speed of Light

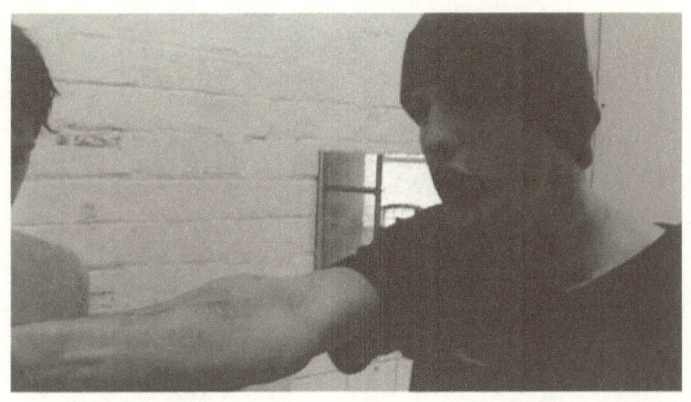

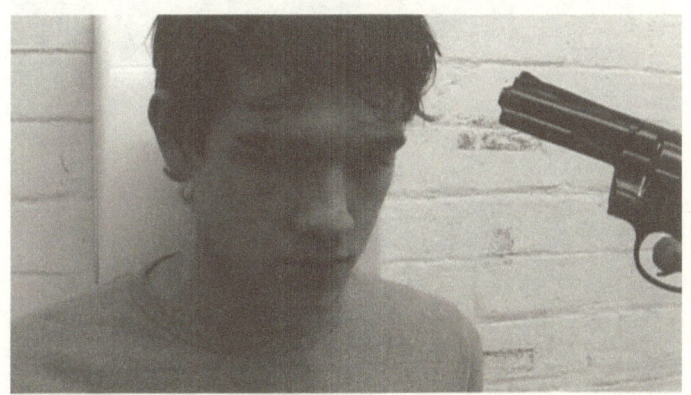

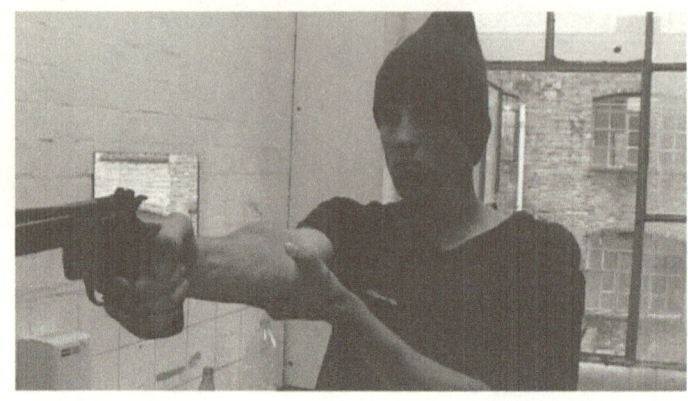

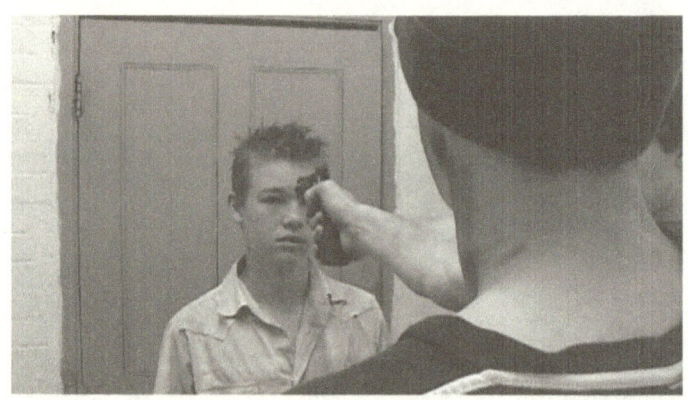

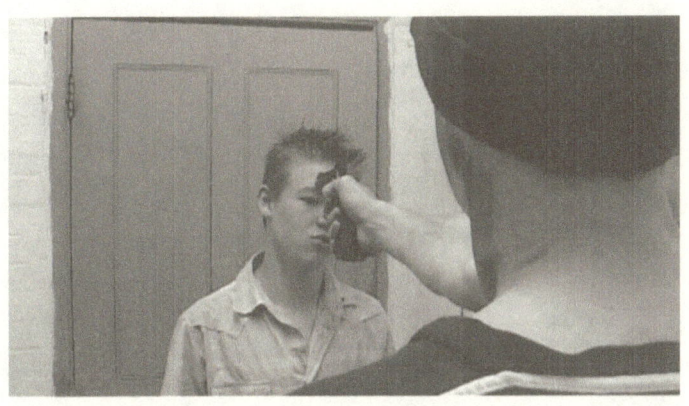

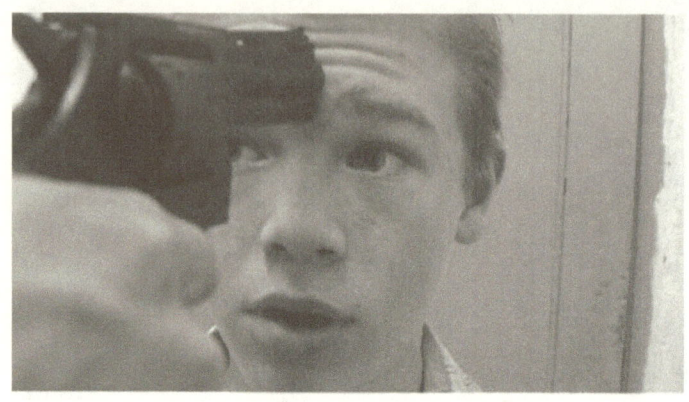

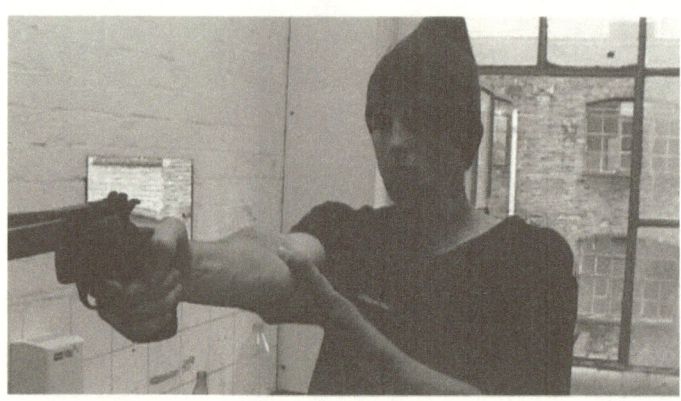

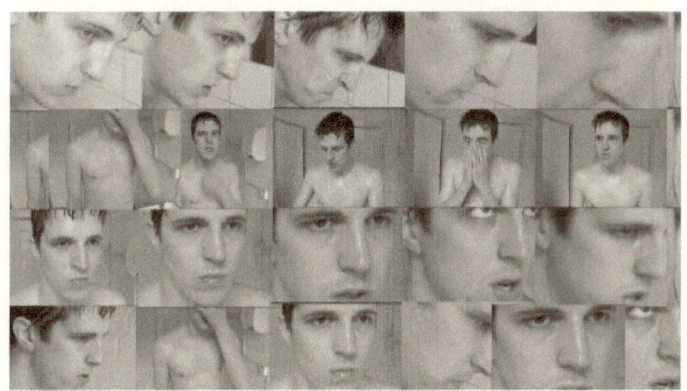

ISBN 978-1-7363620-8-2

Published as a DiaryUnlimited.com paperback by The Edge Press.

www.ingramcontent.com/pod-product-compliance
Lightning Source LLC
Chambersburg PA
CBHW030529260626
47157CB00005B/1951